Kitticorn

Written by **Matilda Rose** • Illustrated by **Tim Budgen**

Sparkle Castle

Rainbow Lake

Twinkle Castle

Fable Fort

Coral Cove

Next time you're in fairyland, make sure you visit Mrs Paws'
Magic Pet Shop in the town of Twinkleton-Under-Beanstalk.
It's truly an enchanting place. There are rainbow rabbits,
playful pugicorns and sparkling seahorses.

One morning, at precisely eleven o'clock, Prince Miles arrived
at the Magic Pet Shop looking for the most perfect pet.

"Good morning, Prince Miles! On time as always!" smiled Mrs Paws.

"I have a busy day ahead," said Miles. "I'm planning an enchanted picnic at Fable Fort tomorrow, so all my friends can meet my new pet!"

MAGIC PET FOOD

MRS PAWS

The
Magic
Pet Shop

To-do list:

9.00: Write to-do list ✔

9.30: Decorate invitations ✔

10.00: Set up picnic benches ✔

11.00: Collect the perfect pet

11.30: Pick up bread from Mr Rye's Bakery

12.30: Make cakes and biscuits

3:00: Collect balloons

4.00: Deliver invitations

5.00: Create party schedule

5.30: Playtime with perfect pet

7.00: Bath and early night

As Miles looked around the shop, one pet immediately caught his eye.

Dozing majestically on
a velvet pillow was . . .
KITTICORN!

She looked as cuddly as a kitten and as graceful as a
unicorn. Kitticorn was perfect for Miles!

"She may look peaceful now, but she's just tired from all the exploring she loves to do!" laughed Mrs Paws.

Kitticorn sleepily nuzzled into Prince Miles. How could something so perfect not be right for him?

Prince Miles set off for Mr Rye's bakery
with Kitticorn napping comfortably in the
basket of his bicycle.

On his way, he spotted Prince Leo
and La-La-Llama making music.

"I can't stop," called Miles, "I have a strict schedule to stick to for the picnic. You'll meet my majestic new pet tomorrow!"

But just then . . .

Kitticorn woke up and leapt straight out of the basket!

She started pawing at the wind chimes, making a terrible racket. Kitticorn wasn't elegant like Miles imagined!

But Leo and La-La-Llama were delighted and began playing
and singing along to the sound of the wind chimes.

"Come and play with us!" said Leo.

"Oh I suppose five minutes won't hurt," said Miles,
as he picked up the tambourine and joined in the fun.

Prince Miles was having so much fun.
But as the clock struck twelve, he realised
Mr Rye would be sold out of fresh bread!

"My whole schedule is messed up
now, Kitticorn! We'll have to bake
the bread ourselves!" cried Miles.

Back at Fable Fort, Miles had to rush
to get all of the food ready.

The cakes were a little messy.   The biscuits were all different sizes.

But the bread looked almost as good as
Mr Rye's! "Maybe we can still have the perfect
picnic, Kitticorn," said Miles, when . . .

Oops! Now the invitations were spoiled . . .

But Miles didn't have time to be cross, so he hopped back on his bike with his very important list.

They collected the balloons and delivered the now-mucky invitations.

"We're nearly back on schedule. Only a few more invites to go—"

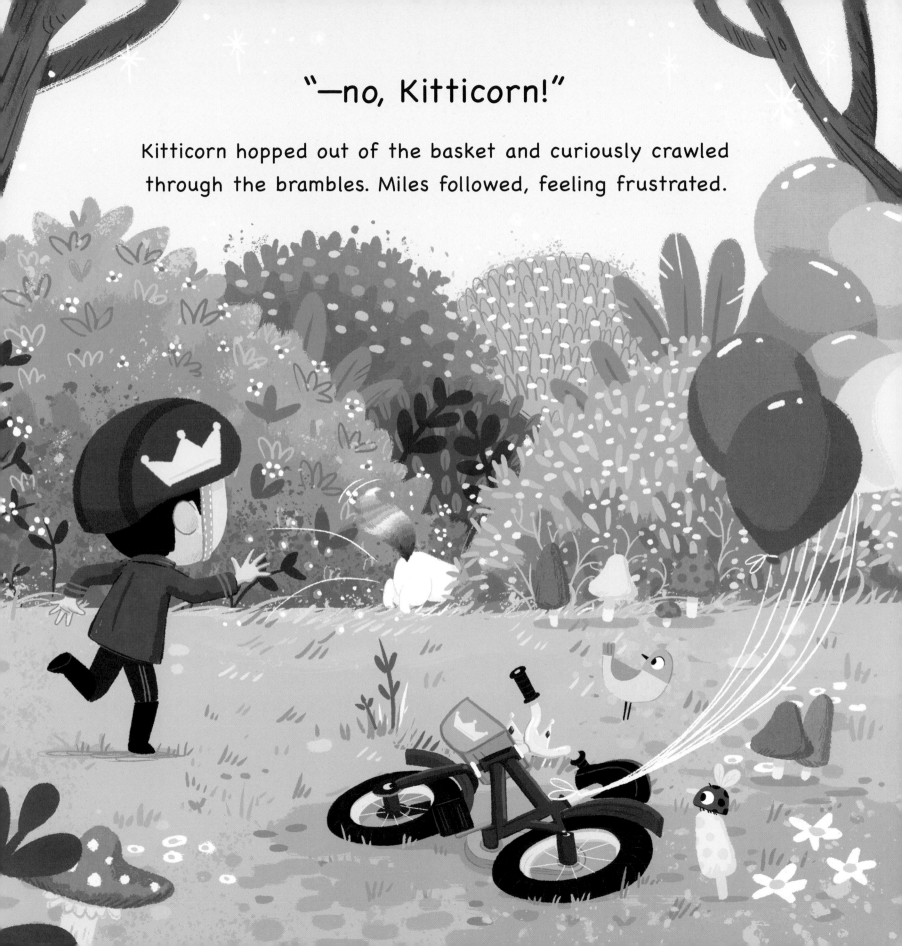

"—no, Kitticorn!"

Kitticorn hopped out of the basket and curiously crawled through the brambles. Miles followed, feeling frustrated.

But as they reached the most magical secret garden, Prince Miles couldn't believe his eyes.

He hesitated. The swing looked like a lot of fun, and Kitticorn was already bounding around making new friends.

"Come and join us!" called Princess Ava.

Miles jumped on the swing, flying higher and higher,
when suddenly he spotted something above . . .

The balloons had blown away into the sky!

"Nothing has gone right since Kitticorn came along," said Miles.
"Here's your invitation, Ava. Sorry it's mucky."

"This is the coolest invitation I've ever seen!" said Princess Ava.
Miles started to smile, feeling a little less cross with Kitticorn.

Back at Fable Fort, Prince Miles planned out his picnic activities to make sure the party would run smoothly.

But he was interrupted again when Kitticorn started pawing at the back door. "ANOTHER adventure?" Miles sighed as he let her outside.

Kitticorn headed straight for her new favourite
tree and as Miles looked up, he saw his balloons!

"They blew all the way across Twinkleton and got
tangled in my tree!" exclaimed Miles.

"Tomorrow will be perfect after all."
Miles gave Kitticorn a scratch behind the ear.
"And soon I'll train you to match my perfect ways!"

The next morning, Prince Miles woke up nice and early to prepare.
But he was faced with yet ANOTHER challenge . . .

"RAIN?" cried Miles. "This wasn't part of the plan!
My enchanted picnic is ruined."

Kitticorn knew how much this picnic
meant to Miles. **She had to do something . . .**

She courageously padded outside, pointed
her rainbow horn to the sky and . . .

WHOOSH!

The rain stopped!

A rainbow of colours beamed across
the sky, and out came the sun!

Prince Miles couldn't believe it. "Kitticorn, you saved my picnic! What would I have done without such a daring pet?"

"I'm sorry I tried to change you, Kitticorn. We had so much fun yesterday because of you, and it didn't matter that we didn't stick to the plan!"

Miles looked at his picnic schedule. It was now a little too muddy for a Perfect Pet Race, and a little too puddly for Musical Bumps.

Picnic Schedule

11.00: Guests arrive
11.15: Biscuits and juice
11.45: Perfect Pet Race
12.15: Pin the Tail on the Unicorn

12.30: Enchanted cake
1.00: Musical Bumps
1.30: Wizard, Wizard, Elf
2.00: Treasure Hunt

Miles ripped it up. "We don't need this list and it doesn't matter if today isn't perfect. With you around, Kitticorn, we're sure to have fun!"

The enchanted picnic was a great success,
even if it involved rain boots and mud pies!

It may not have gone the way Miles had
planned, but, with Kitticorn by his side,
it was the best day ever.

She really was the perfect pet for him.

For Robyn and Ella x
M.R.

Julia, with love x
T.B.

HODDER CHILDREN'S BOOKS

First published in Great Britain in 2021
by Hodder and Stoughton

© Hachette Children's Group, 2021
Illustrations by Tim Budgen

A CIP catalogue record for this book is available from the British Library.

ISBN: 978 1 44495 715 0

1 3 5 7 9 10 8 6 4 2

Printed and bound in China

Hodder Children's Books
An imprint of Hachette Children's Group
Part of Hodder and Stoughton
Carmelite House, 50 Victoria Embankment, London, EC4Y 0DZ

An Hachette UK Company
www.hachette.co.uk
www.hachettechildrens.co.uk